CUMBRIA LIBRARIES

3 8003 04822 9413

KT-547-599

The Princess and the Christmas Rescue

For Louis and Emilia
C.H.

For Dad, who would no doubt find fault in the engineering
S.W.

First published in 2016 by Nosy Crow Ltd
The Crow's Nest, 14 Baden Place,
Crosby Row, London SE1 1YW
www.nosycrow.com

This edition published in 2017
ISBN 978 0 85763 978 3

Nosy Crow and associated logos are trademarks
and/or registered trademarks of Nosy Crow Ltd.

Text © Caryl Hart 2016
Illustrations © Sarah Warburton 2016

The right of Caryl Hart to be identified as the author
and Sarah Warburton to be identified as the illustrator of this work has been asserted.

All rights reserved

This book is sold subject to the condition that it shall not,
by way of trade or otherwise, be lent, hired out or otherwise circulated in
any form of binding or cover other than that in which it is published.
No part of this publication may be reproduced, stored in a retrieval system,
or transmitted in any form or by any means
(electronic, mechanical, photocopying, recording or otherwise)
without the prior written permission of Nosy Crow Ltd.

A CIP catalogue record for this book is available from the British Library.

Printed in China
Papers used by Nosy Crow are made from
wood grown in sustainable forests.

1 3 5 7 9 8 6 4 2

The Princess and the Christmas Rescue

Caryl Hart

Illustrated by Sarah Warburton

nosy crow

On top of the world where the icy winds blow,

A beautiful palace grows out of the snow.

It sits in a forest of towering trees.

The snow is so deep it goes up past your knees.

This wonderful place for just messing about

Was home to a princess who'd never been out.

The king said, "That forest is scary and wild,

With tigers and bears that could eat a small child."

Now, Princess Eliza was brainy and bright.
She kept herself busy from morning till night.
With wood, lots of string and some pieces of wire,
The princess could make anything you'd desire.

ODD-
SOCK-
SORTER

The king said, "This hobby is far from princessy.
Your dress gets so dusty. Your room is so messy."
"It's great that you make all these things," the queen said.
"But how about making a friend now instead?"

"What fun!" thought Eliza. "I'll give it a go.
I'll bake a nice gingerbread boy out of dough."
But when he was cooked, the boy hopped off the tray,
Then stuck out his tongue and . . .

SKEDADDLED away!

Eliza sighed, "I'm getting nowhere like this."
She found a large frog and she gave it a kiss.
She hoped he'd turn into a prince before long.
The frog just said, "Croak," and then . . .

BOING, he was gone!

"Oh well," thought Eliza. "I've plaited my hair.
I'll dangle it out of that window up there.
A knight might climb up – we could have a fun game."
She waited for hours . . . but nobody came.

Poor Princess Eliza looked over the trees
And sniffed at some smoke blowing in on the breeze.
"A frog's not a friend, I can't make one from dough,
And nobody visits because of the snow.

Perhaps there is someone out there I can ask
To help me succeed at this difficult task.
I won't be gone long and I'll wear this warm cloak.
I'll visit whoever is making that smoke."

The princess set off through the glittering frost.

The woods were confusing and soon she was lost.

A huge shaggy shape loomed up out of the snow.

"The tigers and bears," gulped Eliza. "Oh no!"

"Oh, please don't be frightened," a gentle voice said,
And there stood a reindeer with bells on its head.
"I'll take you to safety – just climb on my back.
My master lives down at the end of this track."

Eliza crept in through the open front door,
Past huge sacks of letters piled up on the floor,
And there in a room filled with untidy shelves
Sat a miserable huddle of sad-looking elves.

There was Bertie and Gertie and Felix and Fred,
And Pixie and Dixie and Nora and Ned.
The biggest was Gordon, the smallest was Nell.
Each elf wore a pointed hat topped with a bell.

"Hello?" said Eliza. "I've got a quick question.
How can I make friends? Might you have a suggestion?"
The elves sighed, "Our master is poorly with flu.
We'd all love to chat – but there's TOO much to do."

"We must read these letters, and sort all these toys
To wrap up and give out to good girls and boys."
"I'll help," said Eliza. "I really don't mind."
"There's no point," sighed Bertie. "We're too far behind."

But Princess Eliza knew just what to do:
When the elves went to bed,
she found scissors and glue.

With paper clips, sticky tape,
cardboard and string,
She made a cool gadgety
speed-reading thing.

Next morning, the elves found a neat list of names
That matched every child with the right toys and games.
"Amazing!" cried Felix and Fred in delight.
"Somebody read all those letters last night!"

The elves and Eliza worked hard, side by side.
"This Christmas list goes on for EVER!" Nell cried.
"We'll never get finished before Christmas Day!"
"There, there," said Eliza. "I'm sure there's a way."

That night, young Eliza sprang back into action.
She made a robotic gift-picking contraption.
She flicked the big switch, and in no time at all,
It had all the presents lined up in the hall.

"Bazonkers!" cried Pixie and Dixie next morning.
The elves and Eliza all gathered round, yawning.
"Look! SOMEONE has sorted the toys in the night.
We've checked the list twice, and they've done it just right!"

Then Nora found sticky tape, paper and bows,
But wrapping is tricky, as everyone knows.

The elves and Eliza were doing quite well,
Till Ned cried, "Gadzookers!
We've lost little Nell!"

By bedtime, they'd run out of paper and glue.
"Oh, Princess," said Gordon.
"What ARE we to do?"

"Don't worry," Eliza smiled, rubbing her eyes.
"Perhaps in the morning you'll get a surprise."

And there the next morning, all sparkling and clean,
They found a neat wind-up gift-wrapping machine.
It gave a loud whirr, then a clunk and a hum,
And wrapped all the presents and labelled each one.

"Ho ho!" boomed a voice. "Well, I rather like that!"
And there stood a man in a red suit and hat.
"Oh, SANTA! You're better!" the happy elves cried.
"Your sleigh is all ready to go just outside!"

"A kind person helped us, but no one knows who."
"Princess?" asked Santa. "Could it have been YOU?"
Eliza blushed. "Yes, but don't tell my mum, please.
She said I should stop making gadgets like these."

"What nonsense!" smiled Santa. "I'll give her a ring.
I'm sure she'll be proud. You've done such a great thing.
Now, how do you fancy a magical flight?
Come help me deliver the presents tonight."

The sleigh travelled fast across countries and nations,
All thanks to Eliza's quick modifications.
"We've done it!" beamed Santa. "And super quick, too!
But now it's your turn. What can WE do for YOU?"

"There's ONE thing," Eliza said, blushing bright pink.
"I need a new friend. Could you help, do you think?"
"Oh, Princess," smiled Santa. "Look round and you'll find
You've made LOTS of friends just by being so kind."

The queen heard the news of her daughter's good deeds,
And said to the king, "I know what that child needs."
They sold a few paintings, some clothes and some jewels,
And built her a workshop with all the best tools.

The princess invented a snow-powered sleigh,
And played in the woods with the elves every day.
She helped out each Christmas with kindness and skill,
And as far as I know, she is doing it still!

THE END!